ZED and the Monsters

by Peggy Parish

Paul Galdone
drew the pictures

Doubleday & Company, Inc. Garden City, New York

and the Monsters

Library of Congress Catalog Card Number 77-15876
ISBN 0-385-12948-3 Trade
ISBN 0-385-12949-1 Library

Text Copyright © 1979 by Margaret Parish
Illustrations Copyright © 1979 by Paul Galdone

Meet Zed

A long time ago,

there lived a boy named Zed.

Zed was clever, really clever.

But he was lazy, really lazy.

Zed only worked when his pockets

were empty, plumb empty.

Not one cent in them.

This story is about one of those times.

Zed and Ma

"Well, Ma," said Zed.

"I better find some work."

"I would say so," said Ma.

"Sitting and rocking won't put money

in your pockets."

Zed rocked a little more.

Then he got up.

"I'll get my handy bag," he said.

"Then I'll be on my way."

Zed went to his room.

Ma went to the kitchen.

"I'm packing you a lunch," she called.

"Come and get it."

"All right," called Zed.

He went to the kitchen.

He got his lunch and kissed his ma.

He said, "I'll be back."

"I know that," said Ma.

"Better get going now."

"Reckon so," said Zed.

Zed on the Road

Zed started out. He walked slowly.

"No need to hurry," he said.

"Work will come soon enough."

Zed looked at the sun.

"Eating time," he said.

Zed ate every bite of his lunch.

Then he had a nap.

"Better move on," he said.

Zed stood up.

"Dad zing it!" he said.

"I'm hungry again."

So Zed walked faster.

Soon he saw a big house, biggest he ever s

"Now that's a sight to see," said Zed.

"I'll try my luck here.

That man looks friendly."

Zed Meets the Governor

"Hello there," Zed hollered.

"Hello yourself," hollered the man.

"Come on in."

Zed walked to the house.

"I'm the governor," said the man.

"Pleased to meet you, Mr. Governor,"

said Zed. "I'm looking for work."

"Know anything about monsters?"

said the governor.

"About all there is to know," said Zed.

"Then I've got work for you,"

said the governor. "But first, let's eat."

They went into the kitchen.

Zed's eyes popped open.

He had never seen so much food.

Zed ate his fill.

Then he slipped some grapes and noodles

into his handy bag.

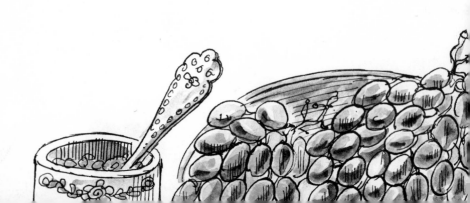

"Now, about those monsters,"

the governor said.

"They are stealing everything from me.

They took all my sheep and cows.

Now they are taking my best trees."

"Are they big?" said Zed.

"Big!" said the governor. "And mean, too!"

"How many monsters are there?" said Zed.

"Four," said the governor.

"Three young ones and an old pa.

I've sent men to get rid of them.

But none ever came back."

Zed listened.

He didn't like what he heard.

The governor said, "Are you scared?"

"Scared! Me scared!" said Zed.

"Shucks, Mr. Governor, nothing scares me.

But Zed was scared.

As scared as he could be.

He wasn't going near any monsters.

Then the governor said,

"If you get rid of those monsters,

I'll fill your pockets with gold."

Zed heard gold. He sat up.

Gold was Zed's magic word.

So he said, "Which way?"

"Just take that road," said the governor.

"They're chopping down my best trees.

You'll see."

Zed Meets Monster One

Zed walked slowly.

"Gold, gold, gold," he kept saying.

Zed was scared. But he wanted that gold.

So he went on.

Later he stopped and looked around.

"Yep," he said. "This is the place."

Zed shook his head.

He said, "First noise I make, they'll come

Better do some thinking."

So Zed did. Then he nodded and said,

"That might work."

Zed found the tallest tree.

He climbed to the tiptop.

Zed got out his ax.

Whack! Whack! Whack!

Zed listened. All was quiet.

Whack! Whack! Whack!

Zed listened again.

Clomp! Clomp! Clomp!

"Who's that?" hollered a monster.

"Me!" hollered Zed.

"Who are you? What are you doing there?" said the monster.

"I'm Zed. I'm getting me some fire wood," said Zed.

He looked down at the monster.

"You're the ugliest thing I ever saw!"

he said.

"And you're a fool," said the monster.

"That's no way to chop fire wood."

"You do it your way. I'll do it mine,"

said Zed.

"Besides, that's my tree," said the monster.

"Not any more," said Zed.

"Come down," said the monster.

"Let's talk this over."

Zed climbed a little lower.

"Come all the way down,"

said the monster.

"Nope," said Zed.

"I said come down," said the monster.

"Nope," said Zed.

The monster got mad, real mad.

He said, "Then I'll chop you down.

And I'll eat you up."

Zed got scared, real scared.

"You hungry?" he said.

"Yes, I'm hungry," said the monster.

"Hungry for you."

"You don't have to chop the tree down,"
said Zed. "I'll give you some of me."

"You will!" said the monster.

"It sure would save me a lot of work."

Zed reached into his handy bag.

Then he dug around his eye.

"Okay," he said. "Here's an eye."

He threw a grape to the monster.

"Good," said the monster. "More."

Zed threw another grape.

The monster ate it up.

"More!" he hollered.

"No more," said Zed.

"I just have two eyes."

"I'm still hungry,"

hollered the monster.

"All right," said Zed.

He dug into his hair with one hand.

He reached into his handy bag

with the other.

"Catch!" he said. "Here's my brains."

The monster caught

a gloppy handful of noodles.

He ate them quickly.

Then he made a face and said,

"I don't like those. I want more eyes."

"Then eat your own," said Zed.

The monster clawed out his eyes.

And then he hollered, how he hollered!

He took off through the woods.

And that was the end of him.

Zed climbed down.

He went to the governor's house.

He told him what the monster did.

Now why did he do a fool thing like that?"

said the governor.

"Just felt like it, I reckon," said Zed.

"Reckon so," said the governor.

Zed and Monsters Two and Three

Zed set out early the next day.

He heard something before he got

to the chopping place.

Whack! Whack! Whack!

Zed started to go back home.

But something inside him said,

"Gold, gold, gold."

So Zed went closer. He saw two monsters.

Ugliest things he had ever seen.

Uglier than the first one.

Then Zed saw a little cave.

Quietly he slipped into it.

Something stuck him. "Ouch!" said Zed.

"What did you say, brother?"

said monster two.

"Huh?" said monster three.

"I didn't say anything."

"Sure thought you did," said monster two.

Zed looked around the cave.

Sharp quills were on the ground.

"A porcupine den!" he said.

Zed thought a bit. Then he said,

"Yep, I'll try that." He opened

his handy bag and found his peashooter.

He put a quill in it. He took aim and blew.

"Ouch!" said monster two.

"Why are you shooting at me?"

"I never shot at you," said monster three.

"Did," said monster two.

"Didn't," said monster three.

"You get that tree chopped."

The monsters started chopping again.

Zed shot another quill.

"OUCH!" said monster two.

"I told you to stop that."

"I didn't do anything," said monster three.

"Oh, hush up," said monster two.

"If you shoot me again, I'll fix you."

They went back to work. Zed waited a bit.

Then he shot another quill.

"OU-CH!" said monster two.

"I told you to stop that."

"I didn't do anything," said monster three.

"You lie," said monster two.

He dropped his ax.

He jumped on monster three.

Those two monsters started to fight.

And what a fight!

The monsters rolled over and over.

Zed came out to watch.

They rolled down a hill still fighting.

SPLASH!

The monsters rolled into the river.

Zed waited and waited.

But they never came up.

So Zed went back to the governor's house.

He told him about the fight.

"Why do you reckon they never came up?"

said the governor.

"Must have gone right through

the river bottom," said Zed.

"Reckon so," said the governor.

Zed and Monster Four

Zed went a new way the next day.

Suddenly something grabbed him

by the shoulder.

Zed looked around.

It was the old pa monster.

Zed shut his eyes.

Nothing could be that ugly.

He opened his eyes and said,

"Yep, I'm seeing right."

"What's your name?" said the old monster

"Zed," said Zed.

"Well, Zed," said the old monster,

"I'm looking for my boys.

Have you seen them?"

"Yep," said Zed. "I saw one running

and hollering in the woods.

Two were in the river."

"I wonder where they went,"

said the old monster.

"I don't know," said Zed.

"Come home with me,"

said the old monster.

"Why?" said Zed.

"I'm hungry," said the old monster.

"I need some food."

That scared Zed, really scared him.

But he couldn't do anything.

That old monster still held him.

So he said, "I'll be glad to help you."

They went to the monster's house.

The old monster looked at Zed.

Then he looked at his stewpots.

"This one looks right," he said.

"Help me get some water."

Zed started thinking,

"I'll soon be in that stewpot."

"Well, come on," said the old monster.

"Coming," said Zed.

They went to the river.

Zed was thinking all the time.

Suddenly he started jumping up and dow

"What's wrong with you?"

said the old monster.

"I'm just happy," said Zed.

"An old friend of mine lives around here."

Zed hollered, "Hey, friend!"

Then he said, "Did you see?

He's in the river.

He just poked his head out of the water."

"I didn't see anything," said the old monster.

"Just hope he didn't see you!" said Zed.

"He doesn't like many people," said Zed.

"He's big, real big, and he loves to fight."

The old monster looked and he looked.

But he still didn't see anything.

"My eyes must be going bad," he said.

"You want to see his picture?" said Zed.

"Yes," said the old monster.

Zed reached into his handy bag.

He pulled out a mirror

that made things look real big.

He handed it to the old monster.

Zed said, "That's him."

"Oh no!" said the old monster.

"I never saw anything so big and ugly.

Please don't call him out."

"Yep," said Zed. "I want to see him.

He'll come out if I ask him to."

"Please, Zed," said the old monster.

"Don't call him yet. The train's coming soon.

Let me get on it."

"Better hurry," said Zed.

"I want to see my friend."

That old monster took off.

He made it just in time.

Zed saw him jump on top of the train.

So Zed went back to the governor's house.

He told him what the old monster did.

"Why do you reckon he did that?"

said the governor.

"Reckon he thought it was time to move on,"

said Zed.

"Reckon so," said the governor.

"I do thank you, Zed."

"Shucks," said Zed. "That was easy."

"Tomorrow I'll give you more work,"

said the governor.

"Hold it, Mr. Governor," said Zed.

"My pockets want to feel that gold."

So the governor filled every pocket Zed had,

and his handy bag, too.

Zed didn't know there was that much gold

in the world.

That night Zed slipped out

and headed for home.

"Ma will sure be glad to see me," he said.

"It will be a long time

before my pockets are empty again.

Ma can have all the fancy things

she wants."

Zed walked faster.

His rocking chair was waiting for him.

And Zed was in a hurry to keep it company.